MARVEL

GUARDIANS OF THE GALAXY

ROCKET AND GROOT FIGHT BACK

Adapted by Adam Davis
Illustrated by Ron Lim, Drew Geraci, and Lee Duhig
Based on the Screenplay by James Gunn
Story by Nicole Perlman and James Gunn
Produced by Kevin Feige, p.g.a.
Directed by James Gunn

LB

LITTLE, BROWN AND COMPANY
New York Boston

marvelkids.com

Little, Brown and Company

Hachette Book Group
237 Park Avenue, New York, NY 10017
Visit our website at lb-kids.com

Little, Brown and Company is a division of Hachette Book Group, Inc.
The Little, Brown name and logo are trademarks of Hachette Book Group, Inc.

The publisher is not responsible for websites (or their content) that are not owned by the publisher.

First Edition: July 2014

Library of Congress Control Number: 2014937168

ISBN 978-0-316-29323-5

10 9 8 7 6 5 4 3 2 1

CW

Printed in the United States of America

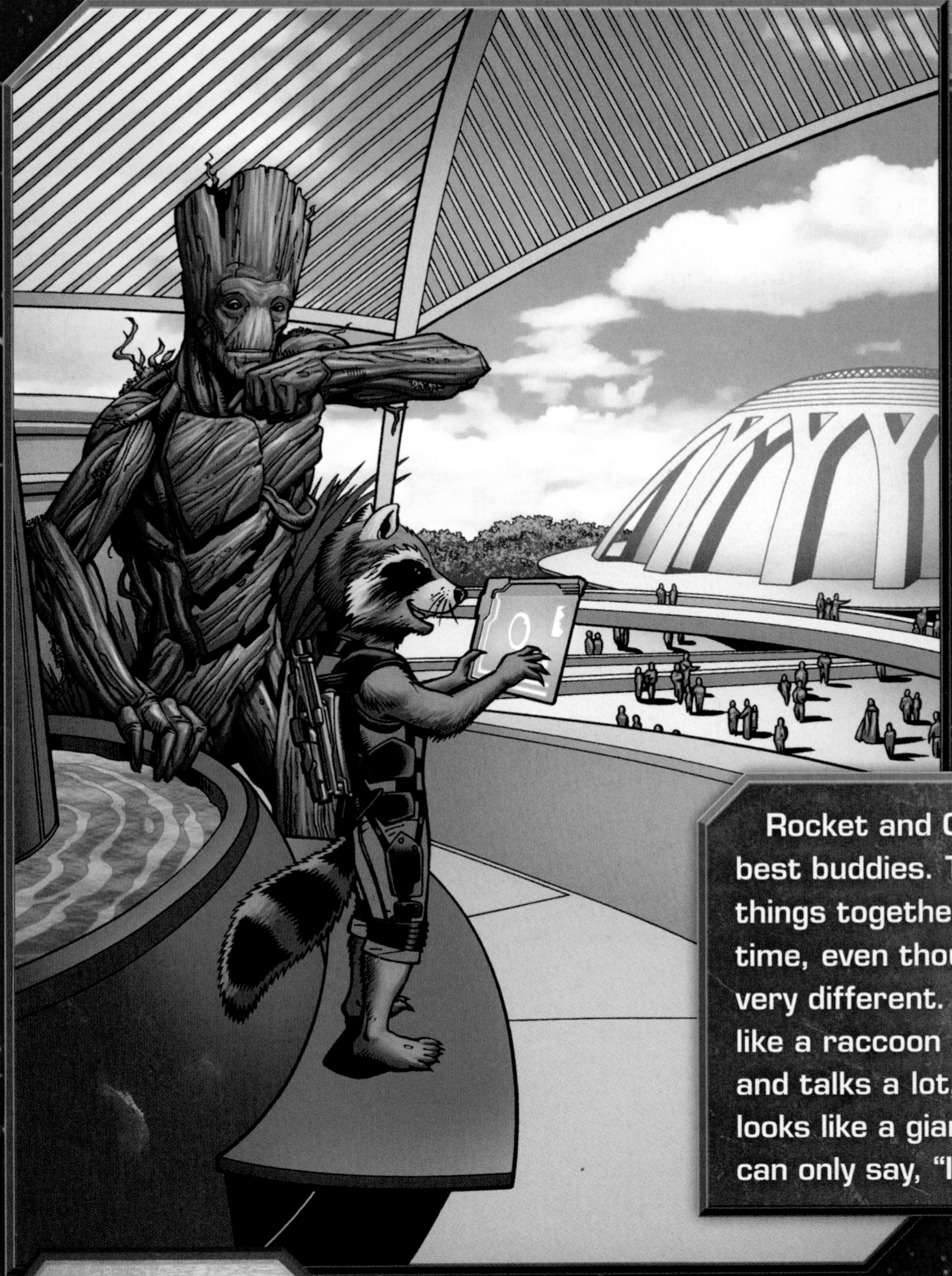

Rocket and Groot are best buddies. They do things together all the time, even though they are very different. Rocket looks like a raccoon from Earth and talks a lot, while Groot looks like a giant tree and can only say, "I am Groot."

One day, while hanging out at the mall, the friends see a green-skinned woman get into a fight with a man. Suddenly, the woman takes a shiny ball from him and runs!

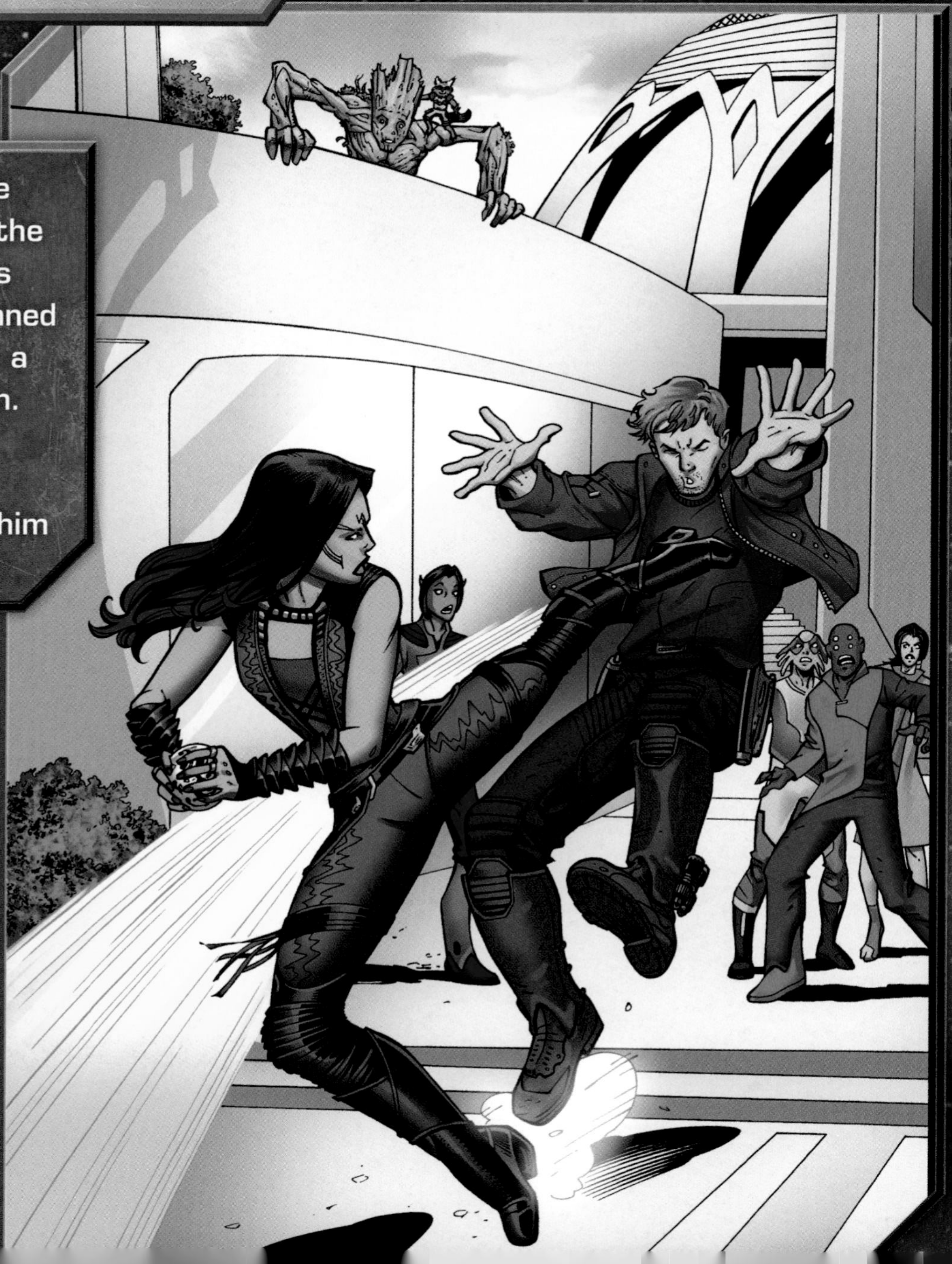

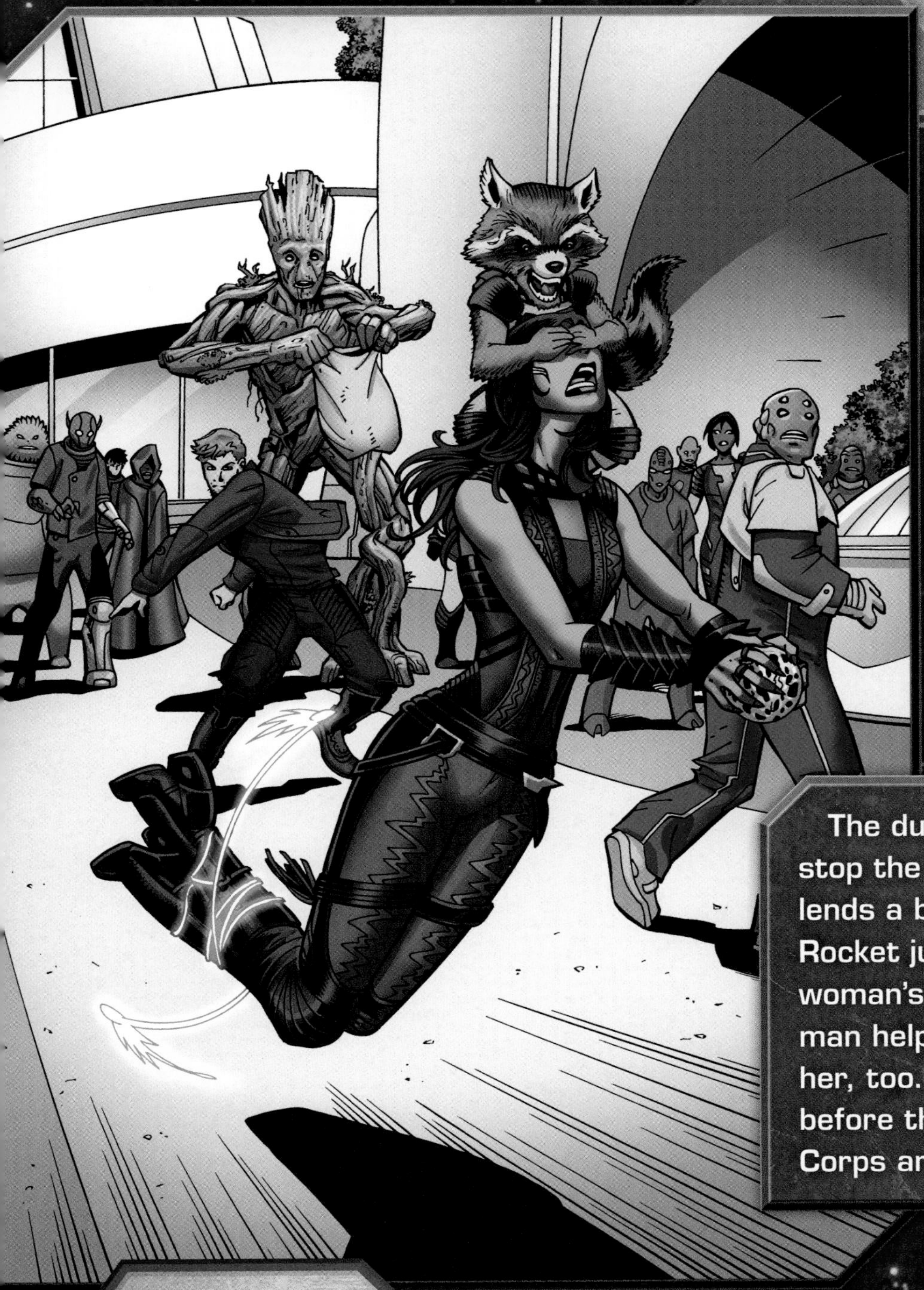

The duo must stop the thief! Groot lends a branch as Rocket jumps on the woman's head. The man helps catch her, too. It isn't long before the Nova Corps arrive!

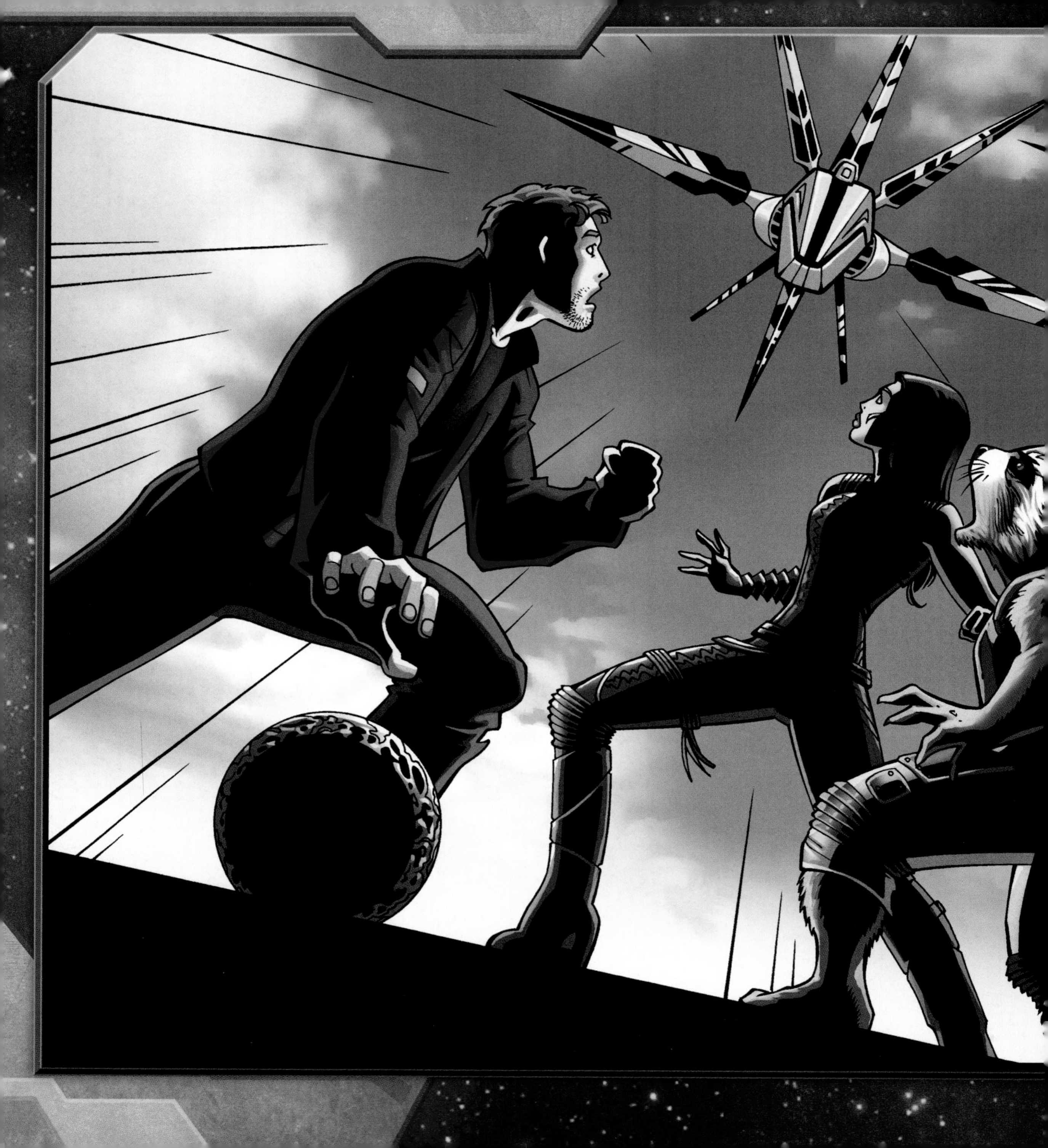

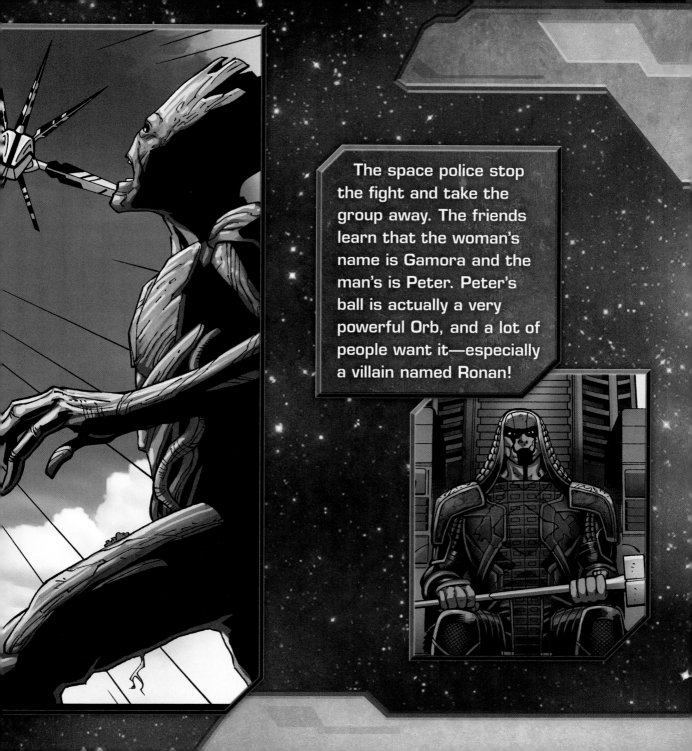

The space police stop the fight and take the group away. The friends learn that the woman's name is Gamora and the man's is Peter. Peter's ball is actually a very powerful Orb, and a lot of people want it—especially a villain named Ronan!

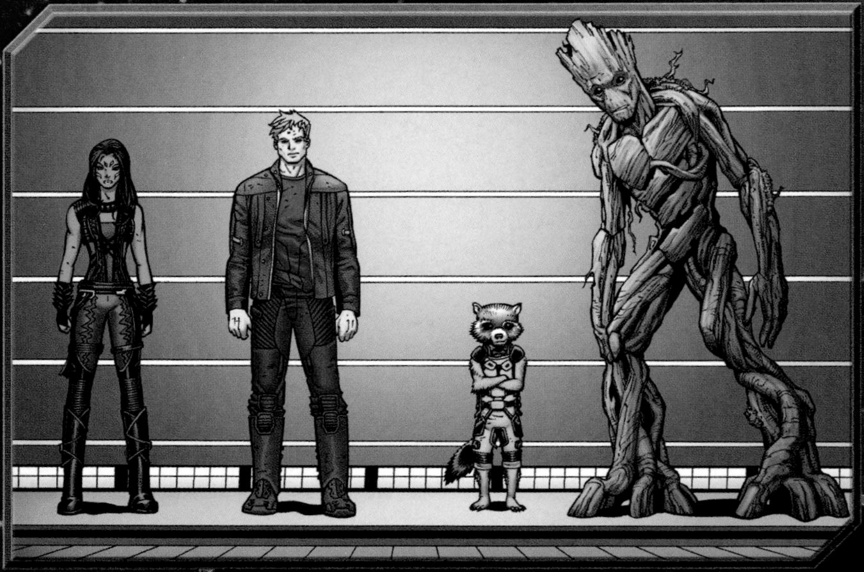

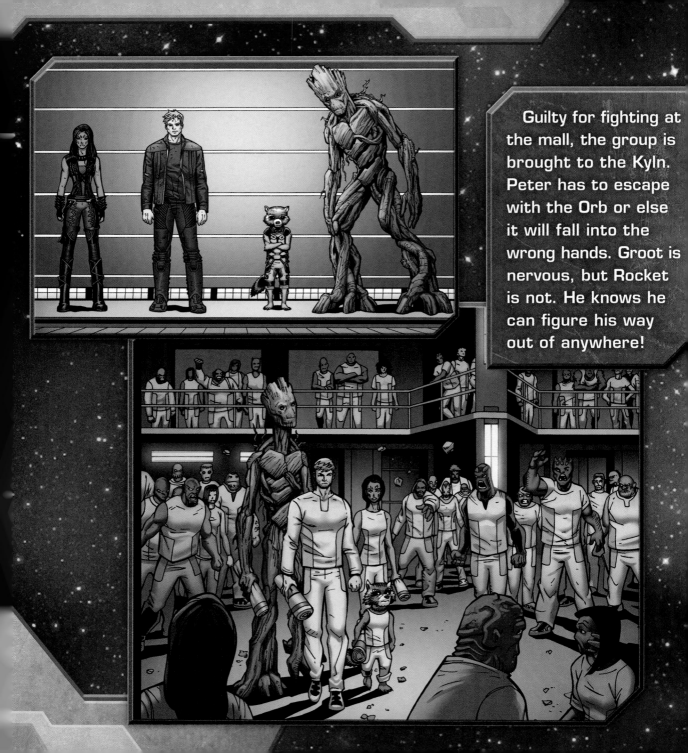

Guilty for fighting at the mall, the group is brought to the Kyln. Peter has to escape with the Orb or else it will fall into the wrong hands. Groot is nervous, but Rocket is not. He knows he can figure his way out of anywhere!

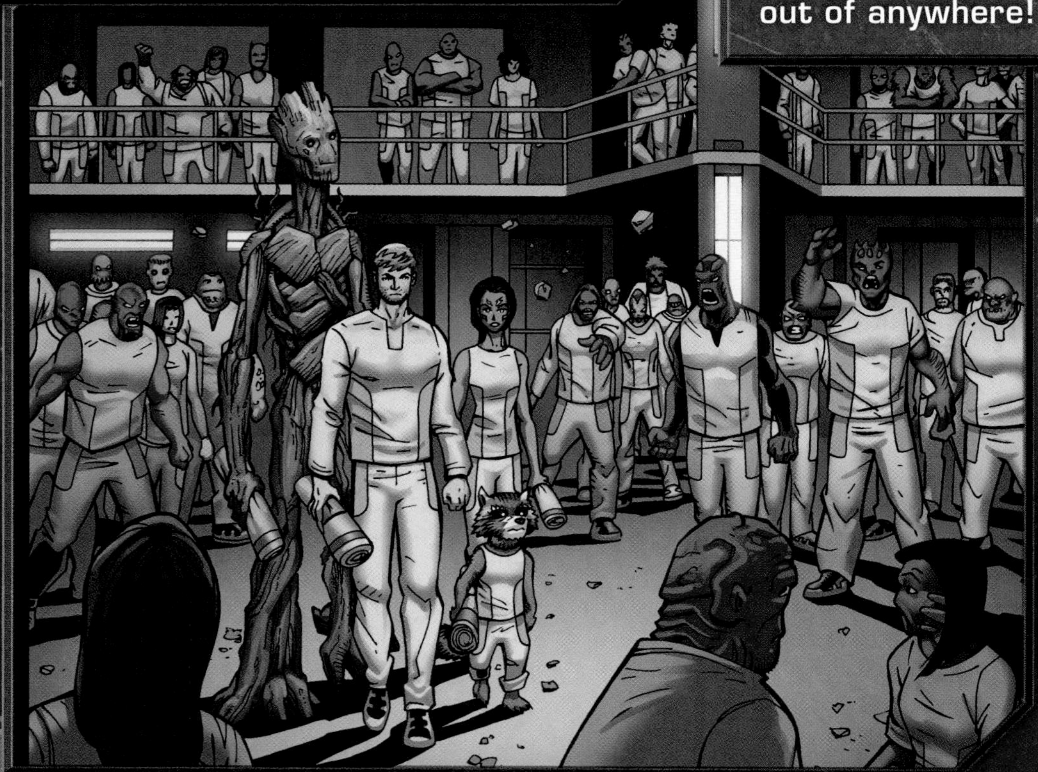

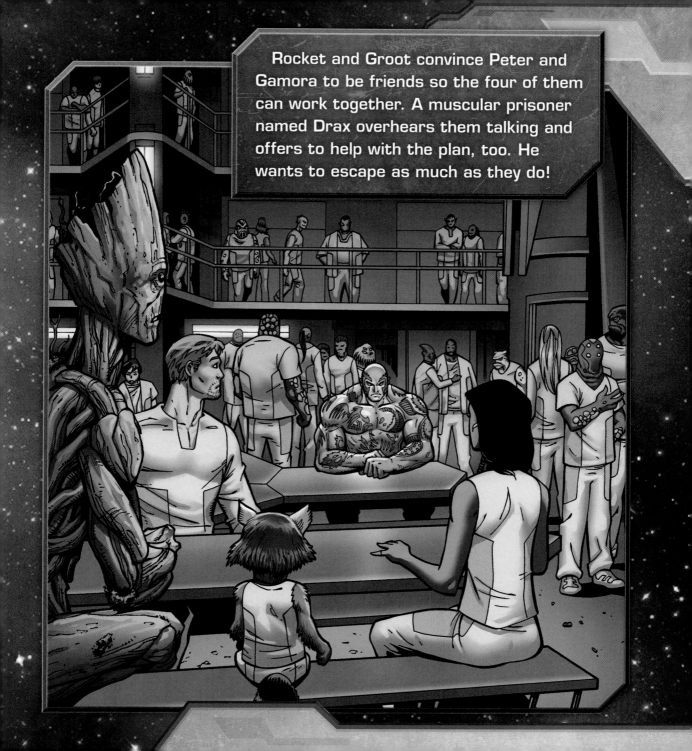

Rocket and Groot convince Peter and Gamora to be friends so the four of them can work together. A muscular prisoner named Drax overhears them talking and offers to help with the plan, too. He wants to escape as much as they do!

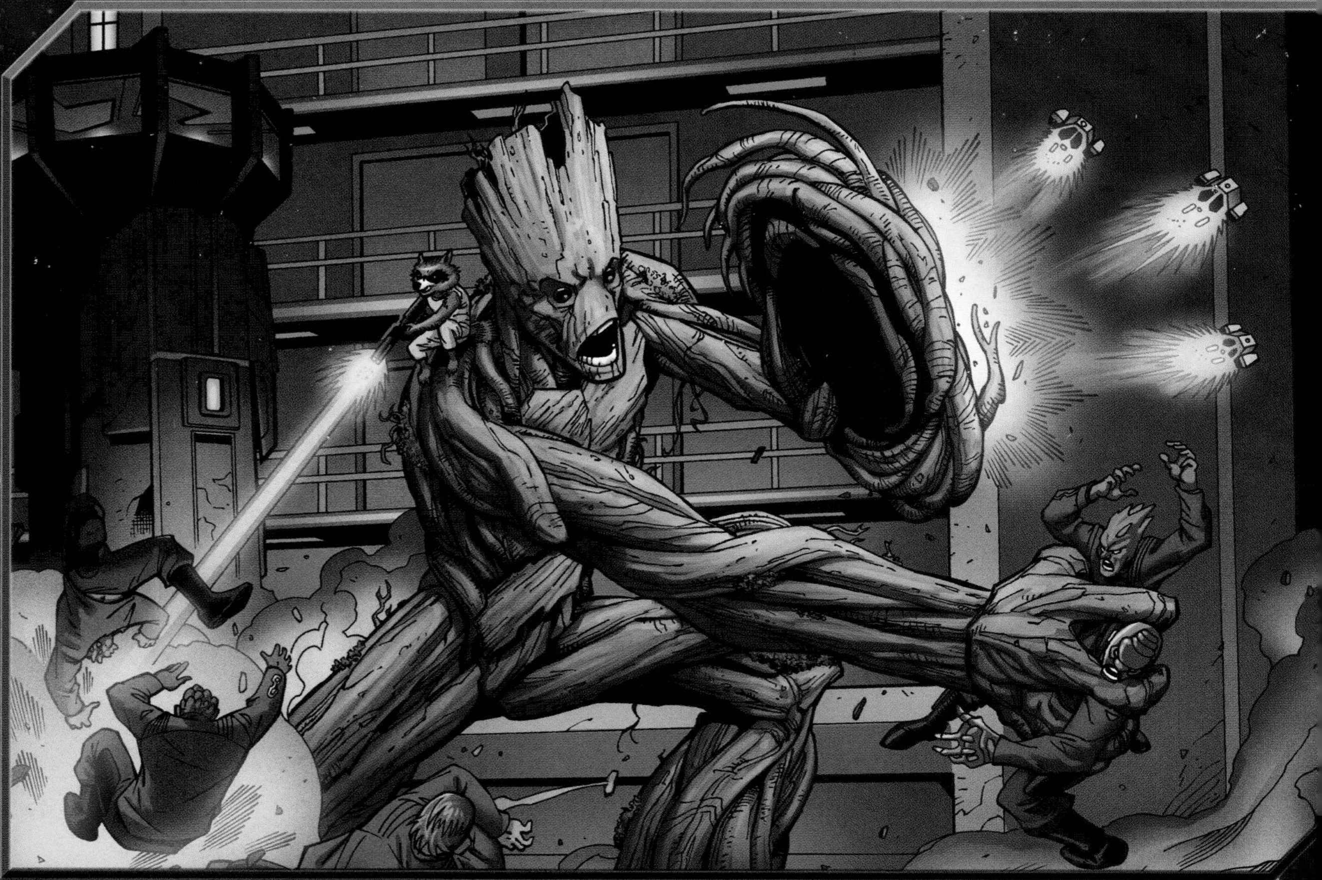

Soon Rocket has a plan! He tells Groot to grow to twice his size and smash the flying robot guards. Rocket rides on his shoulder, keeping other foes away.

Peter, Gamora, and Drax fight bravely, as well. They throw powerful kicks and punches!

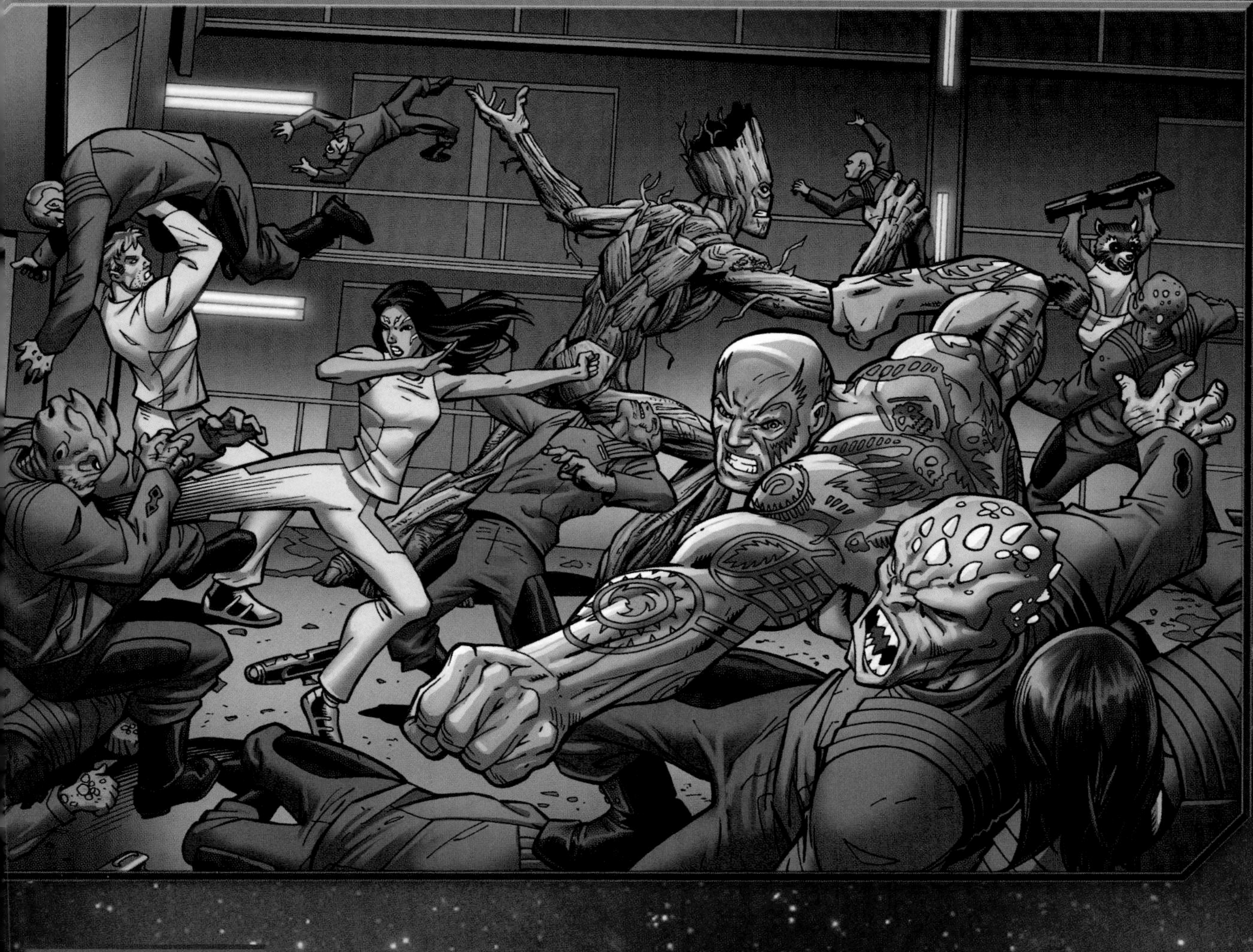

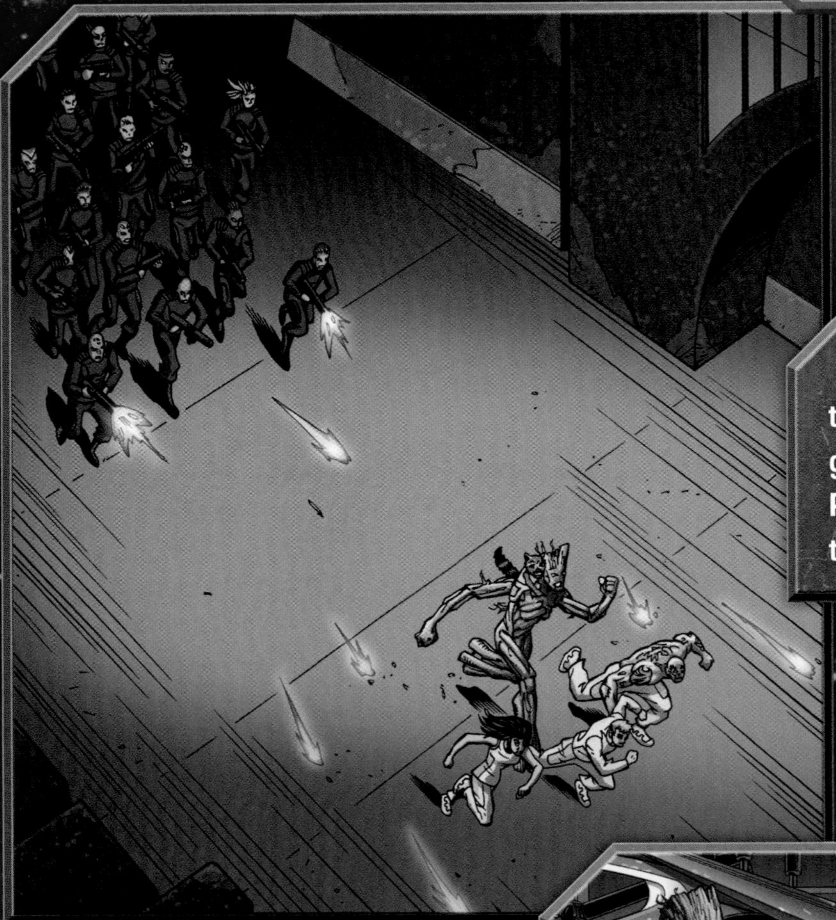

After getting the Orb back, the group runs to Peter's spaceship, the *Milano*.

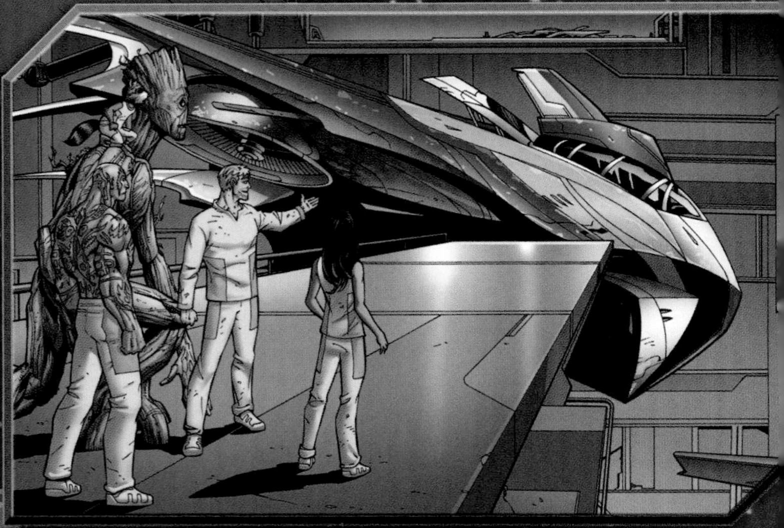

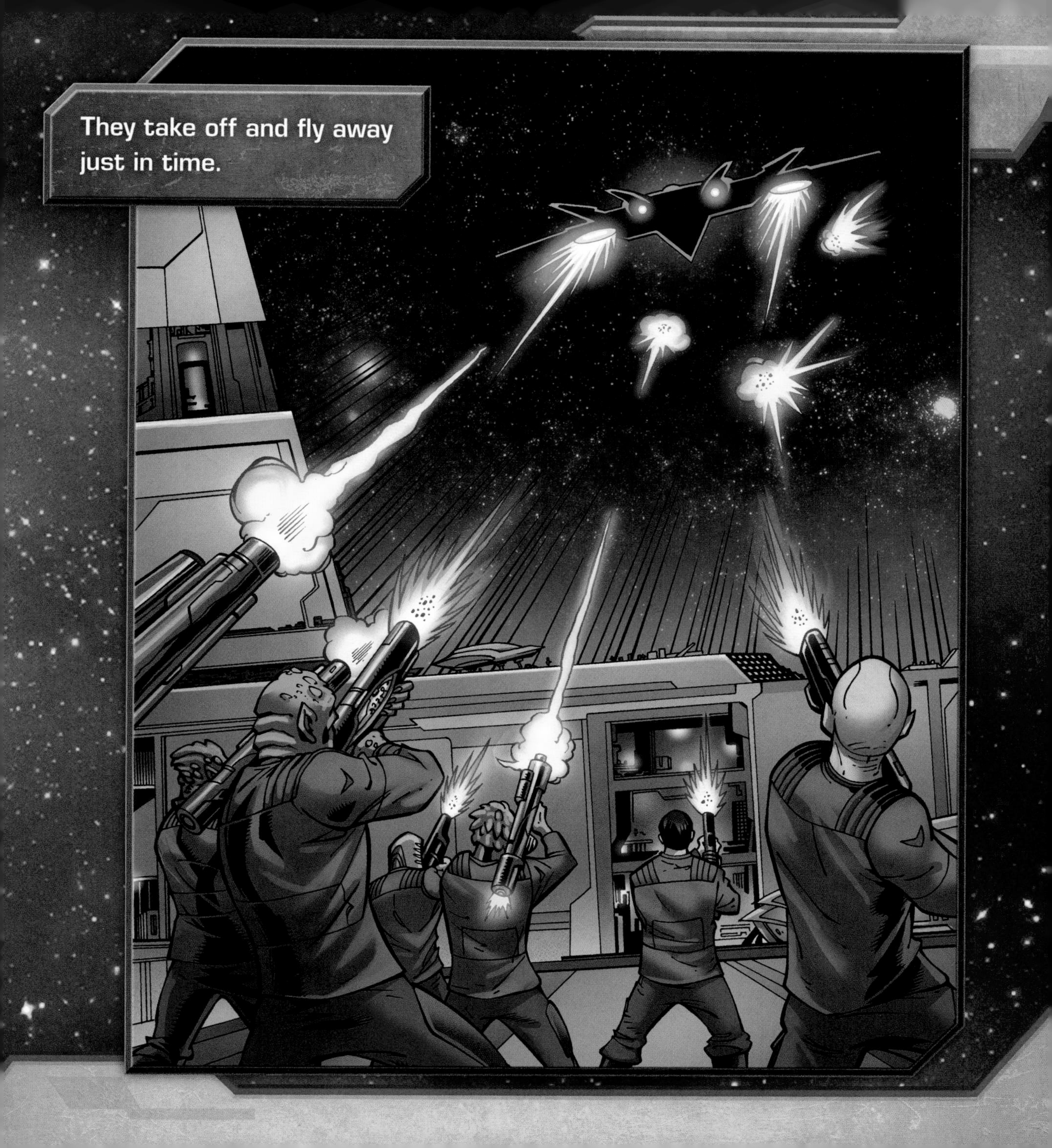
They take off and fly away just in time.

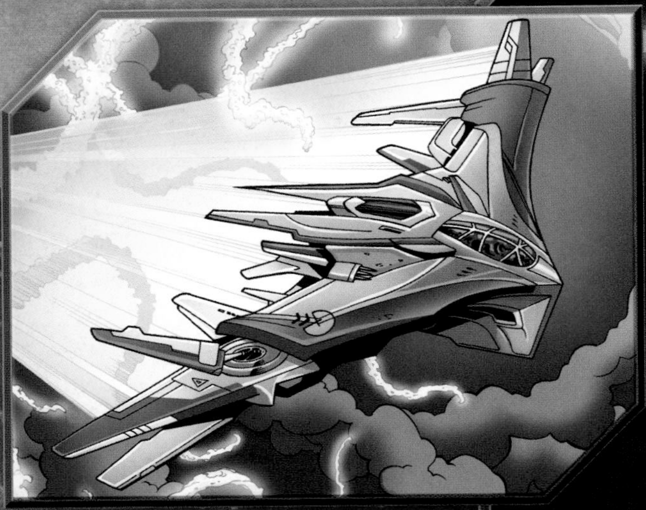

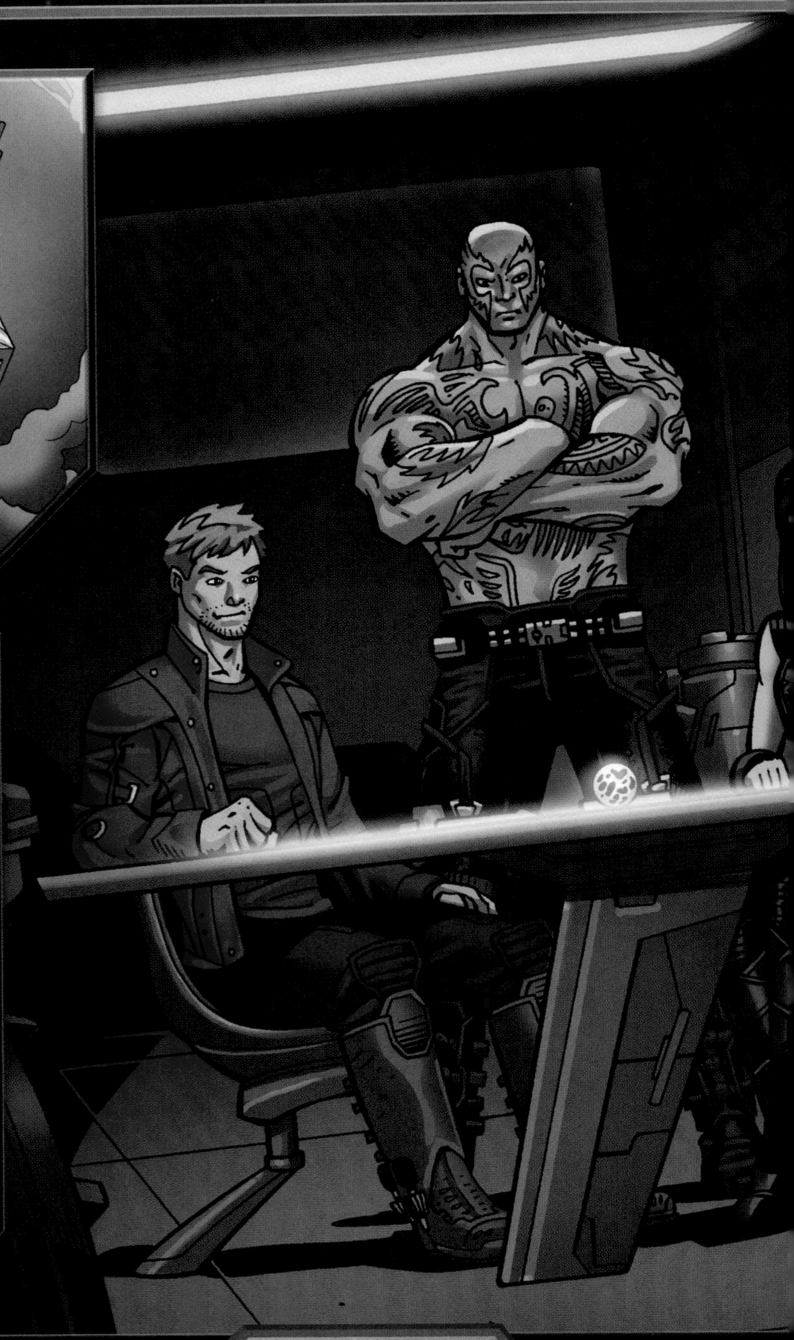

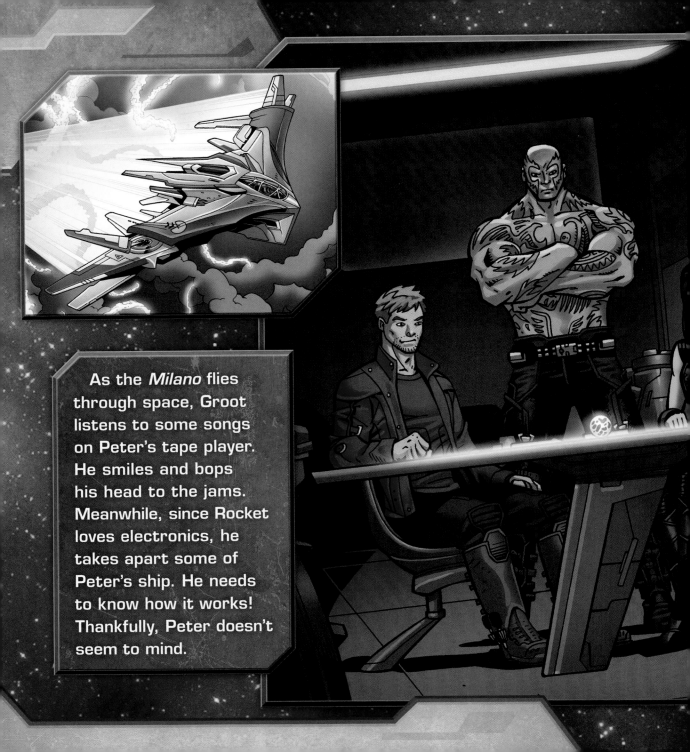

As the *Milano* flies through space, Groot listens to some songs on Peter's tape player. He smiles and bops his head to the jams. Meanwhile, since Rocket loves electronics, he takes apart some of Peter's ship. He needs to know how it works! Thankfully, Peter doesn't seem to mind.

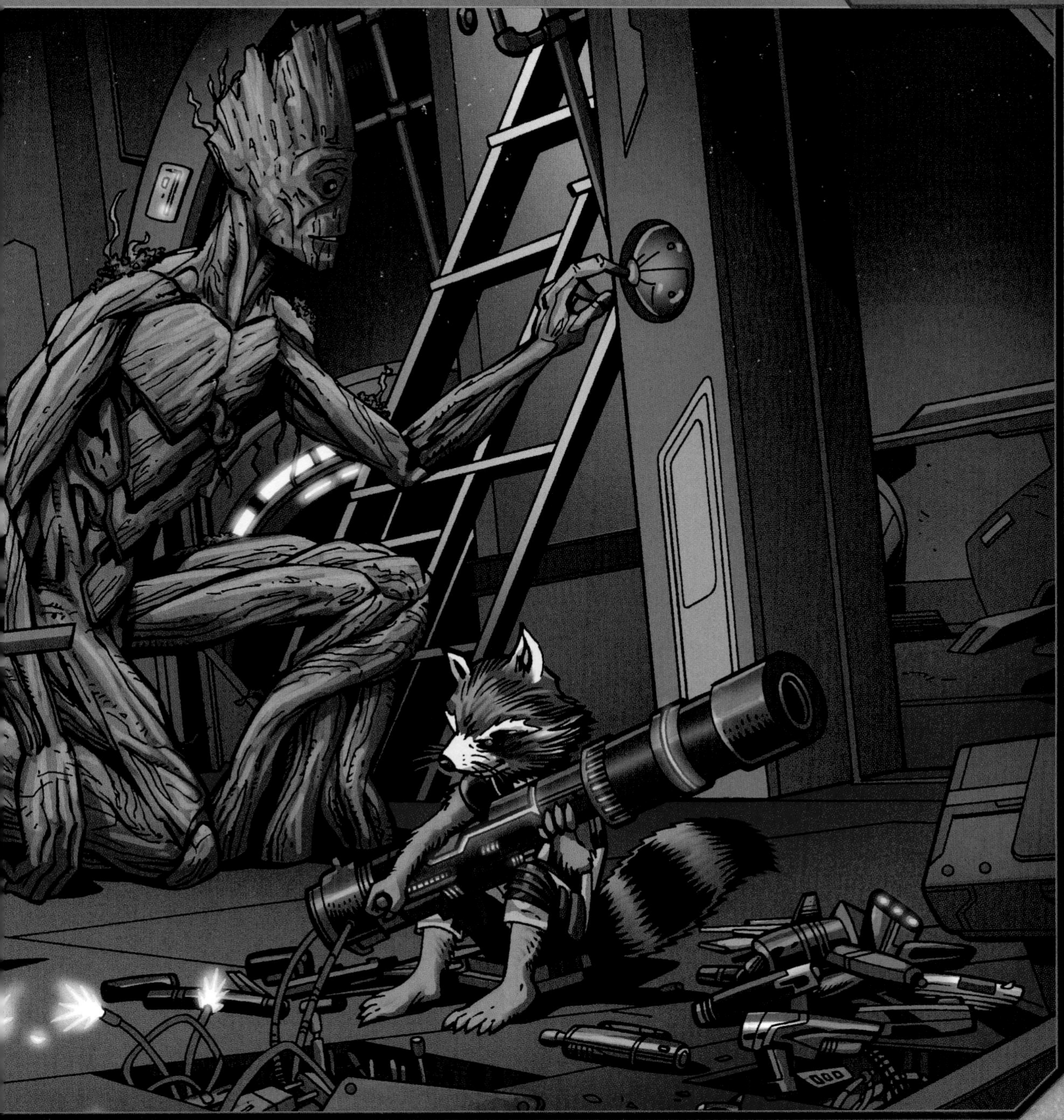

After a few hours, the group lands on a place called Knowhere. There are so many strange-looking species of plants and animals in all shapes and sizes; Rocket and Groot are amazed at the sights.

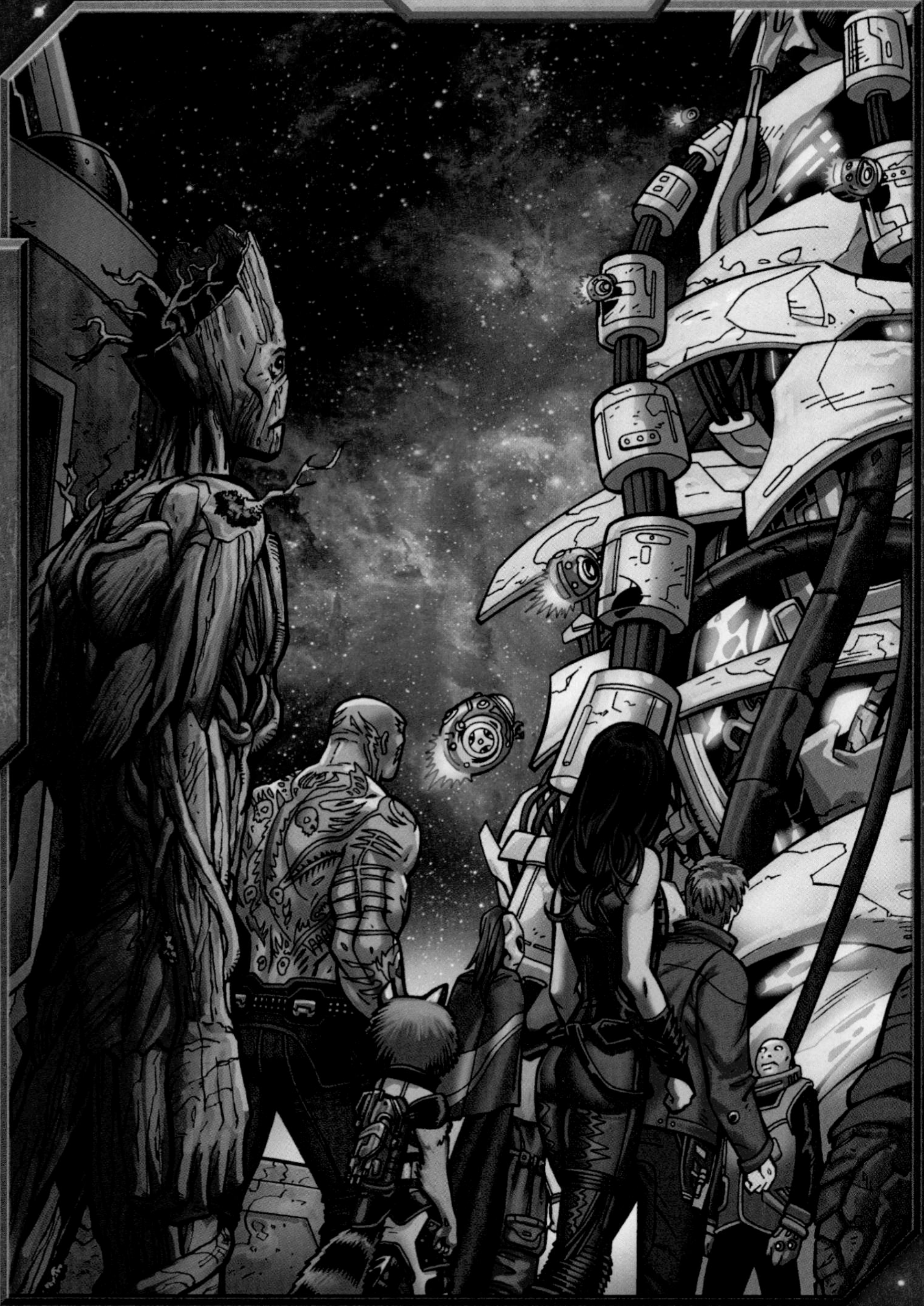

While Peter and Gamora take the Orb to the Collector, who can tell them more about it, Rocket and Groot decide to have some fun. They cheer on racing Orloni along with Drax. Groot has never seen a sport like this, though, and he thinks it's weird.

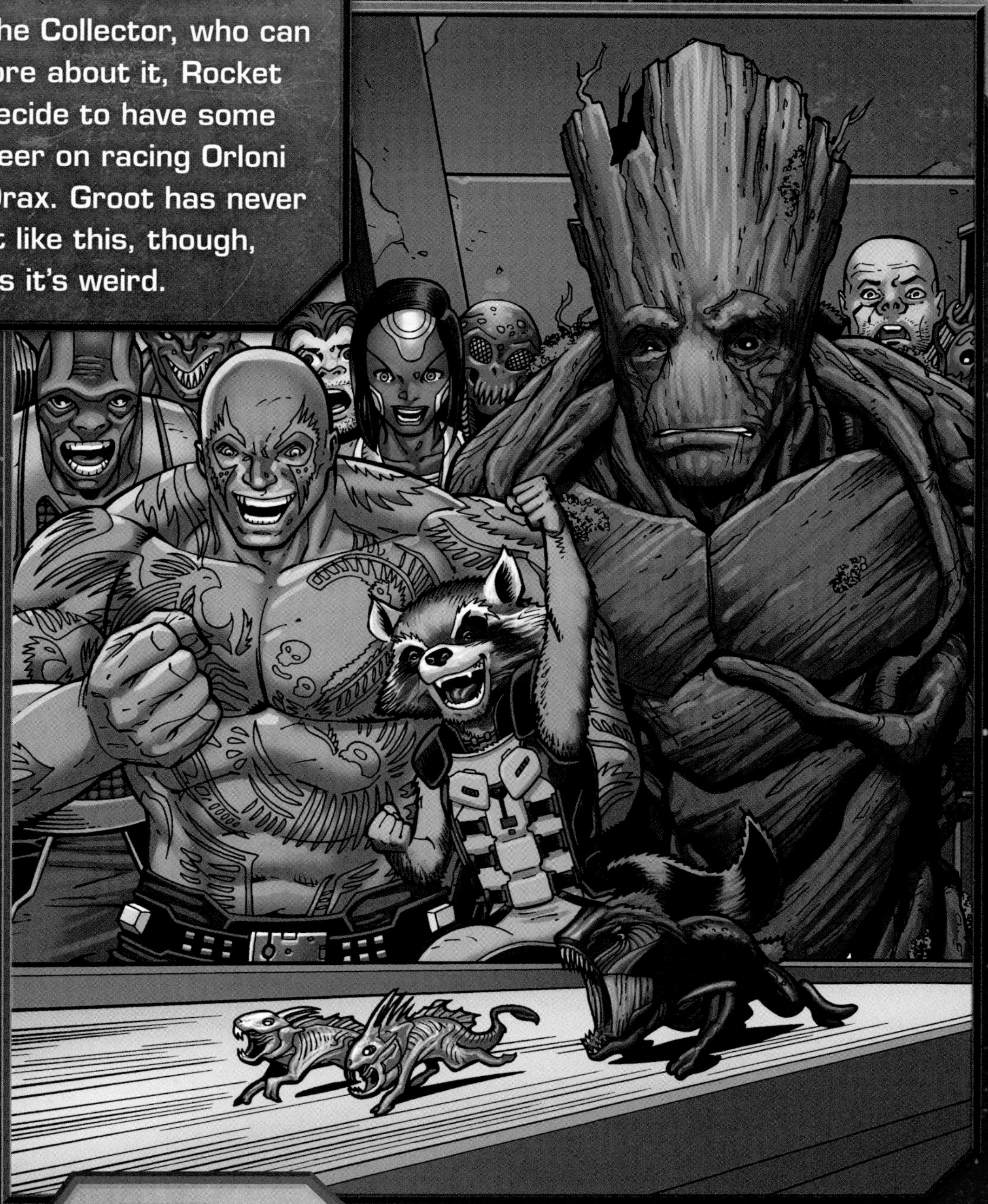

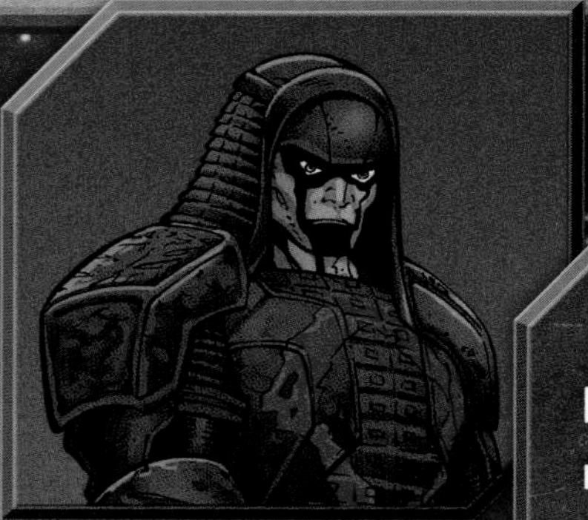

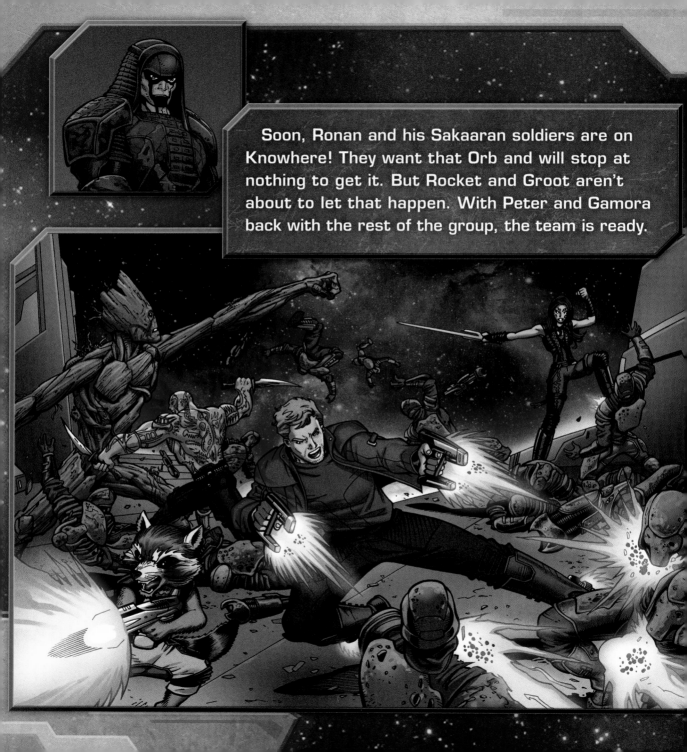

Soon, Ronan and his Sakaaran soldiers are on Knowhere! They want that Orb and will stop at nothing to get it. But Rocket and Groot aren't about to let that happen. With Peter and Gamora back with the rest of the group, the team is ready.

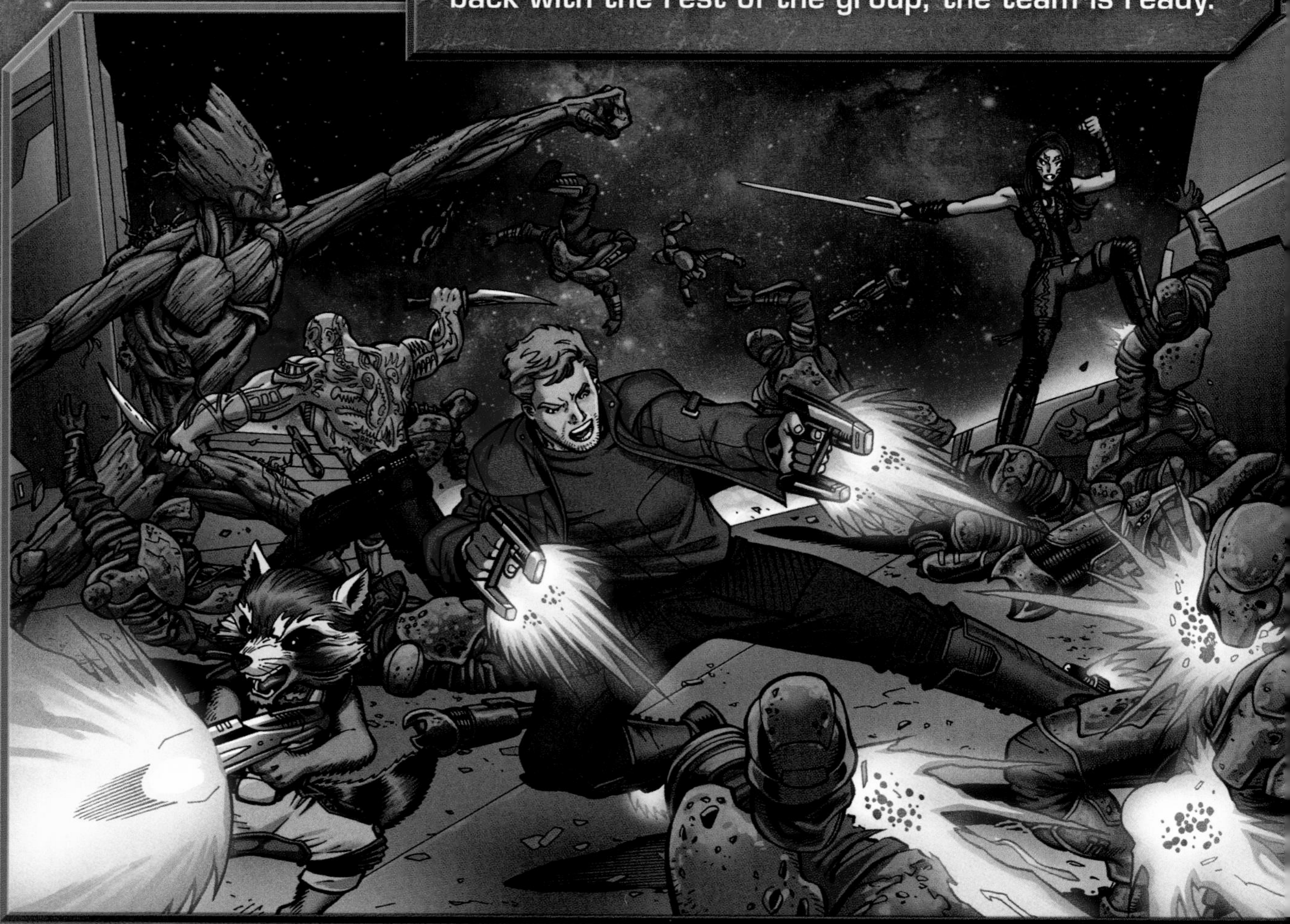

Rocket and Groot take on the troops alongside their new friends.

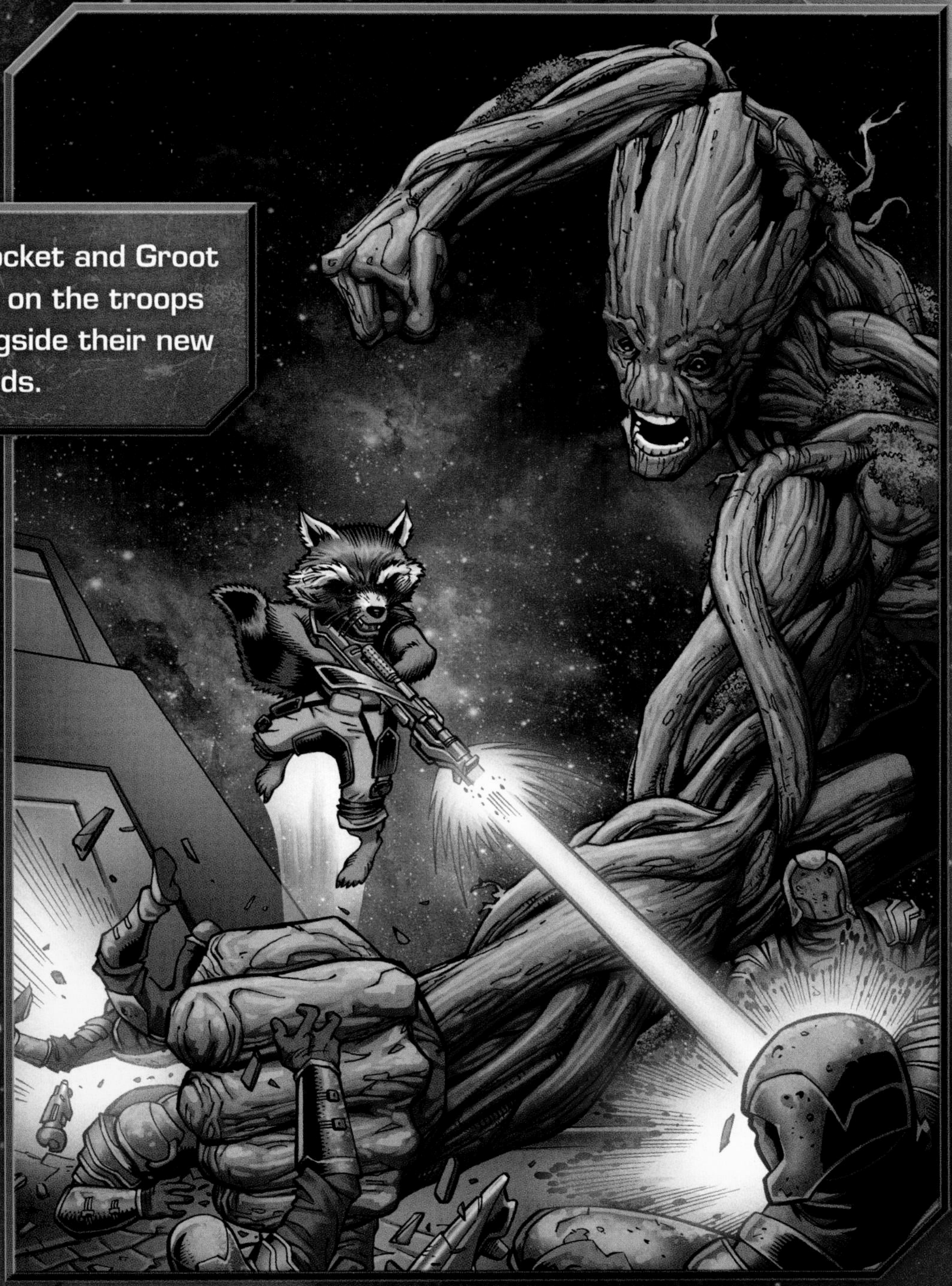

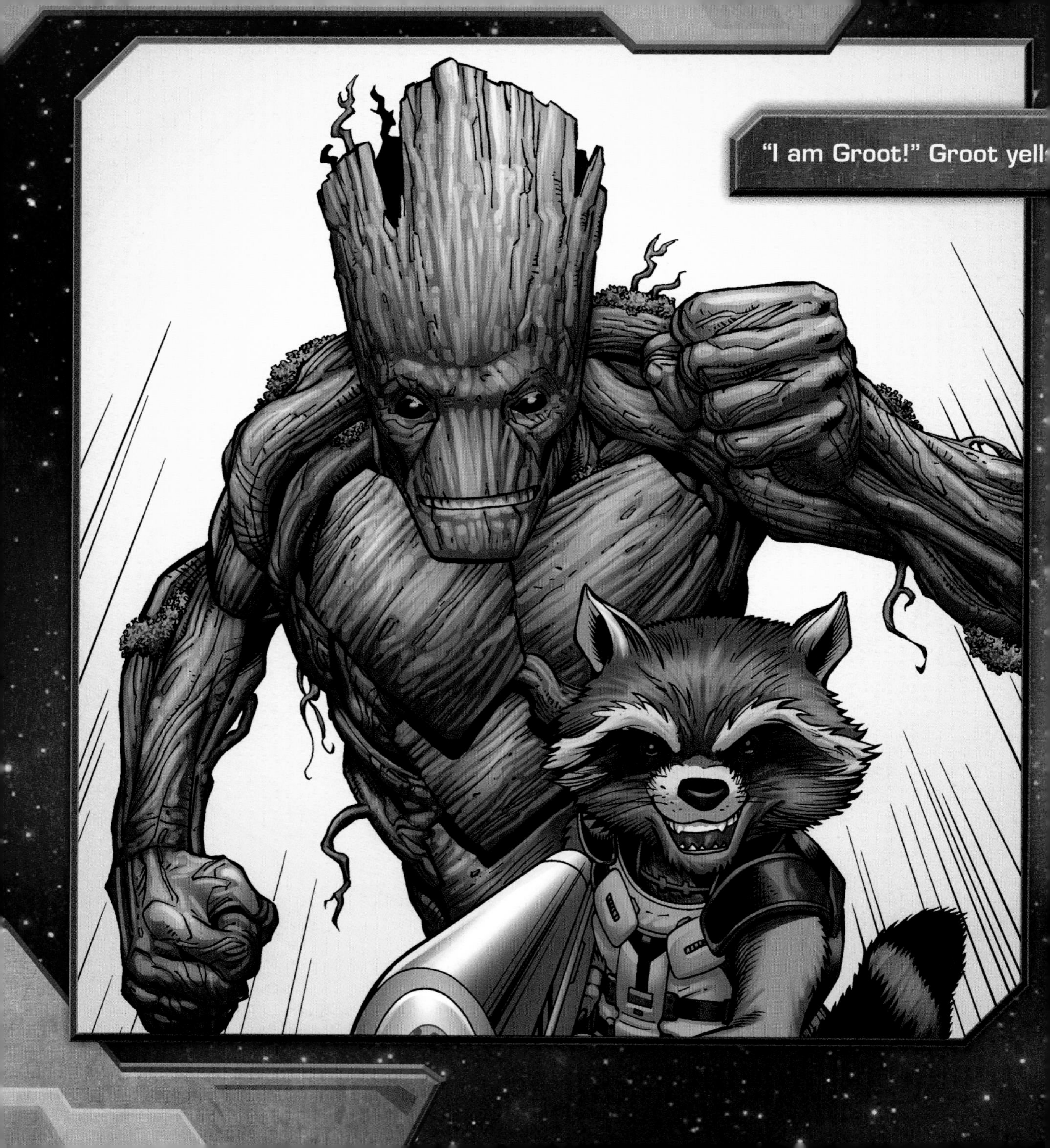

“I am Groot!” Groot yell

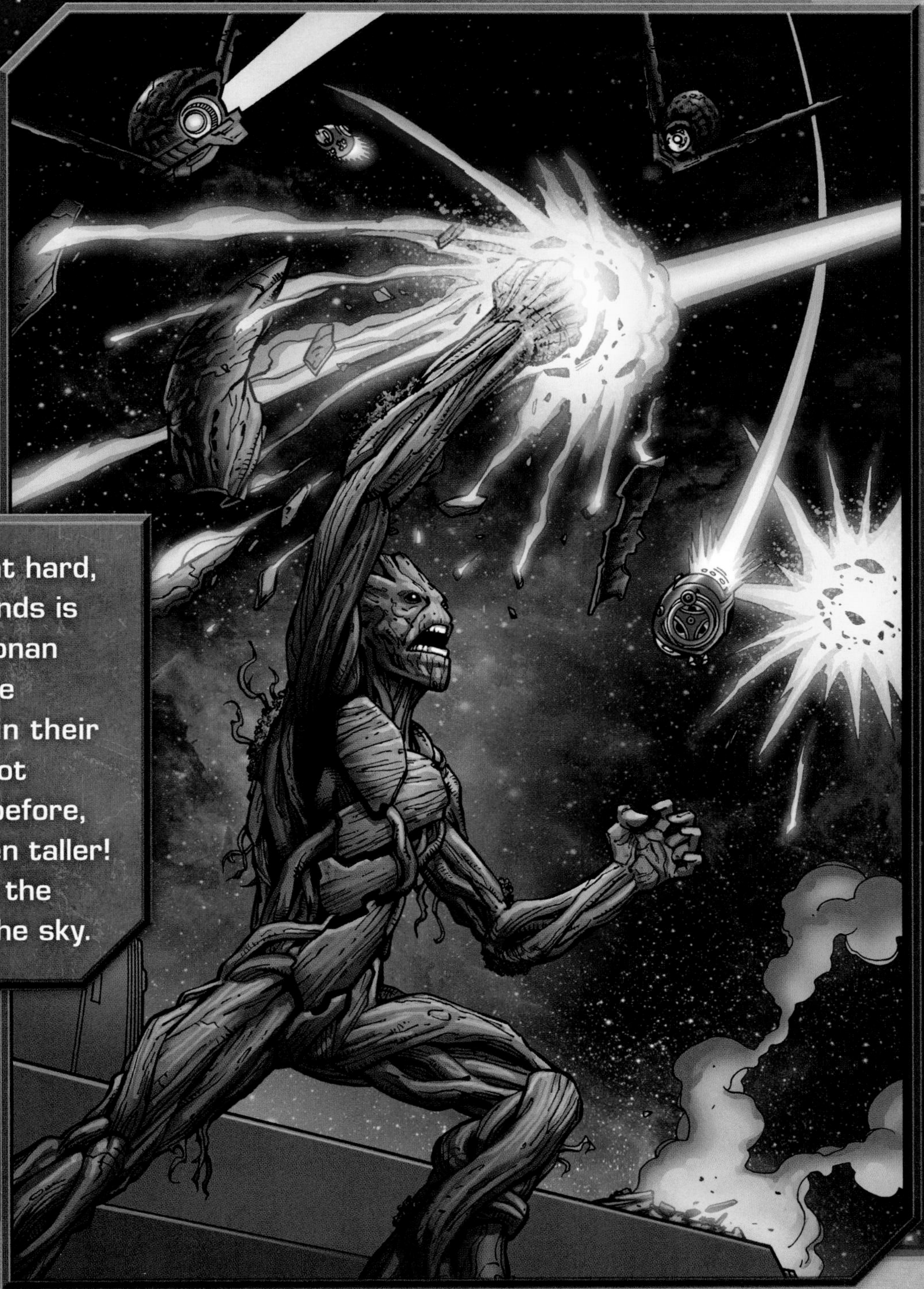

While they fight hard, the group of friends is outnumbered. Ronan gets the Orb! The villains take off in their spaceships. Groot grows, just like before, but this time even taller! He tries to swat the enemies out of the sky.

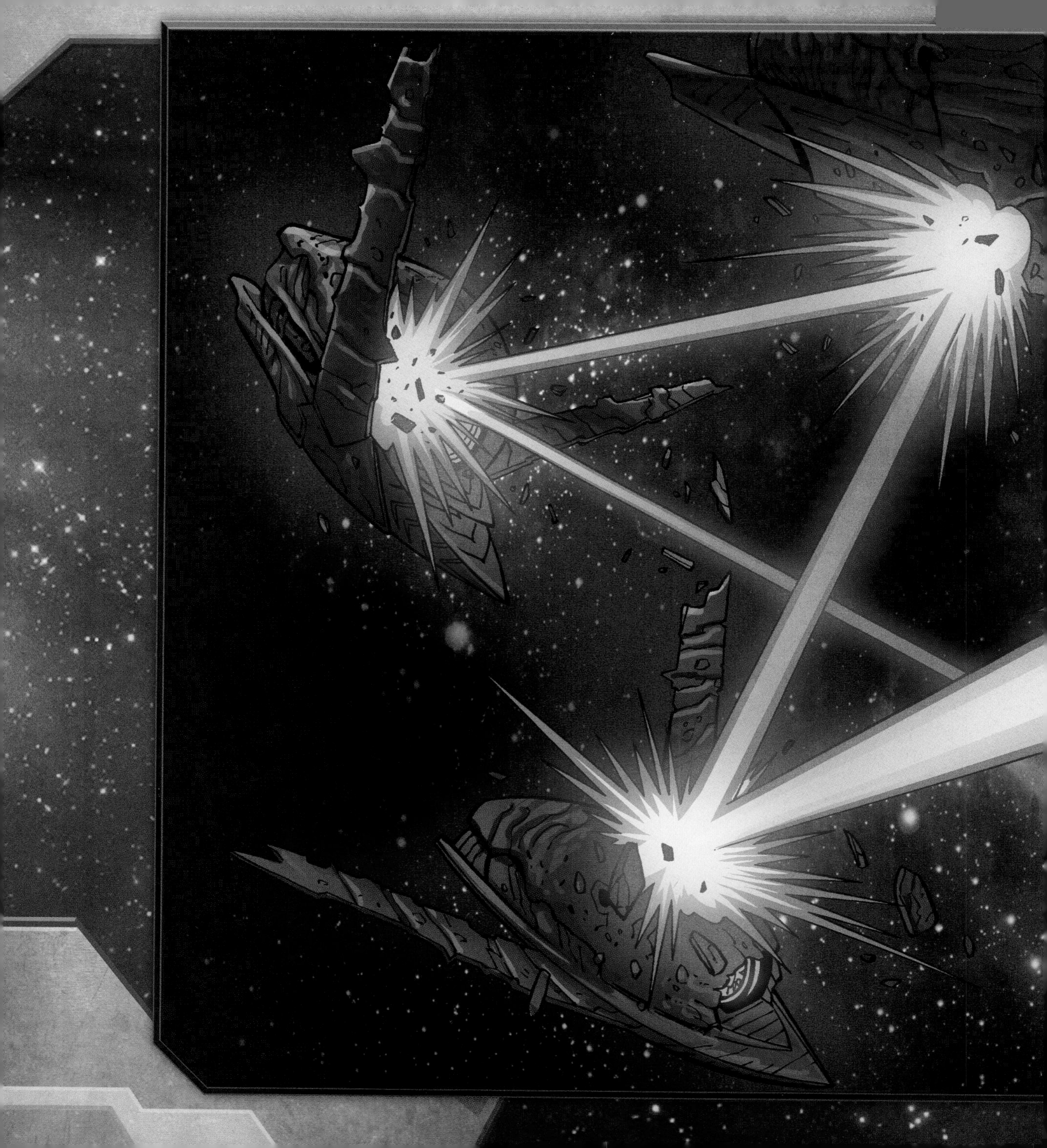

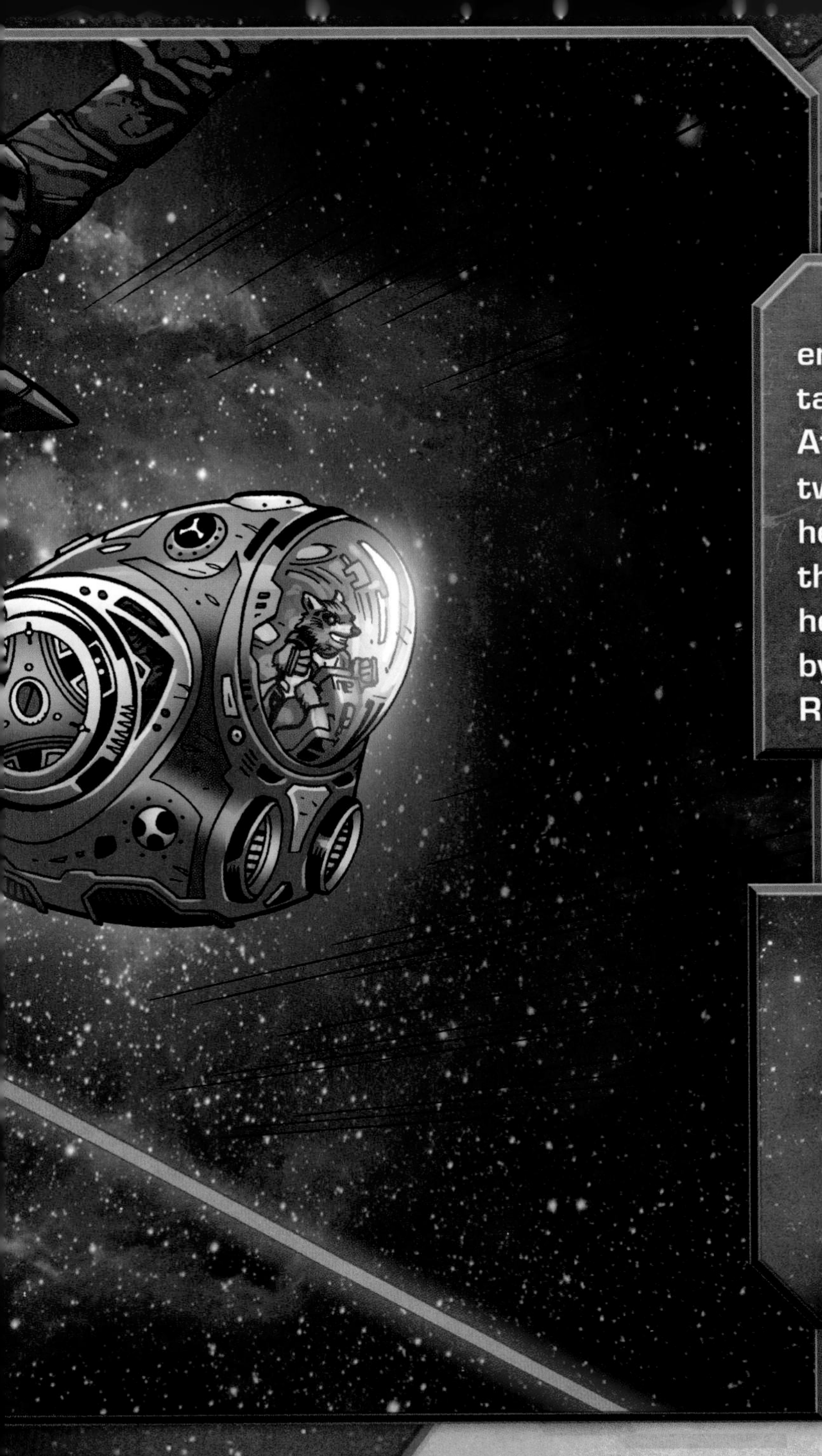

Rocket hops into an empty spaceship and takes off after Ronan. After smashing through two Sakaaran ships, he's close to reclaiming the Orb! But just then he's outmaneuvered by another ship, and Ronan gets away!

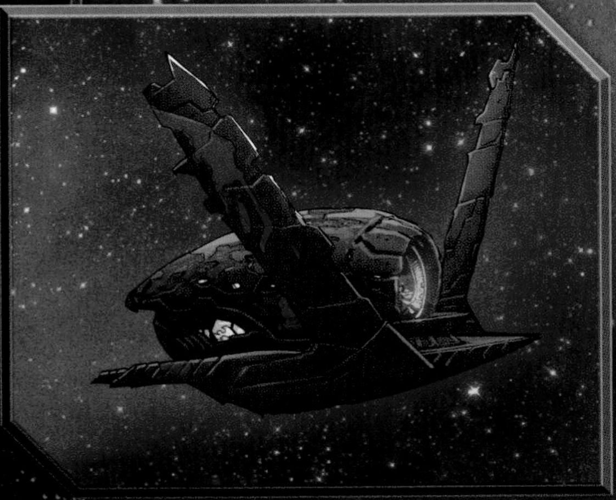

Back on the ground, Rocket and Groot are disappointed. But then they look over at Peter, Gamora, and Drax. Even though they lost the Orb to Ronan, they made new friends. More important, they're ready to keep fighting—as the Guardians of the Galaxy!

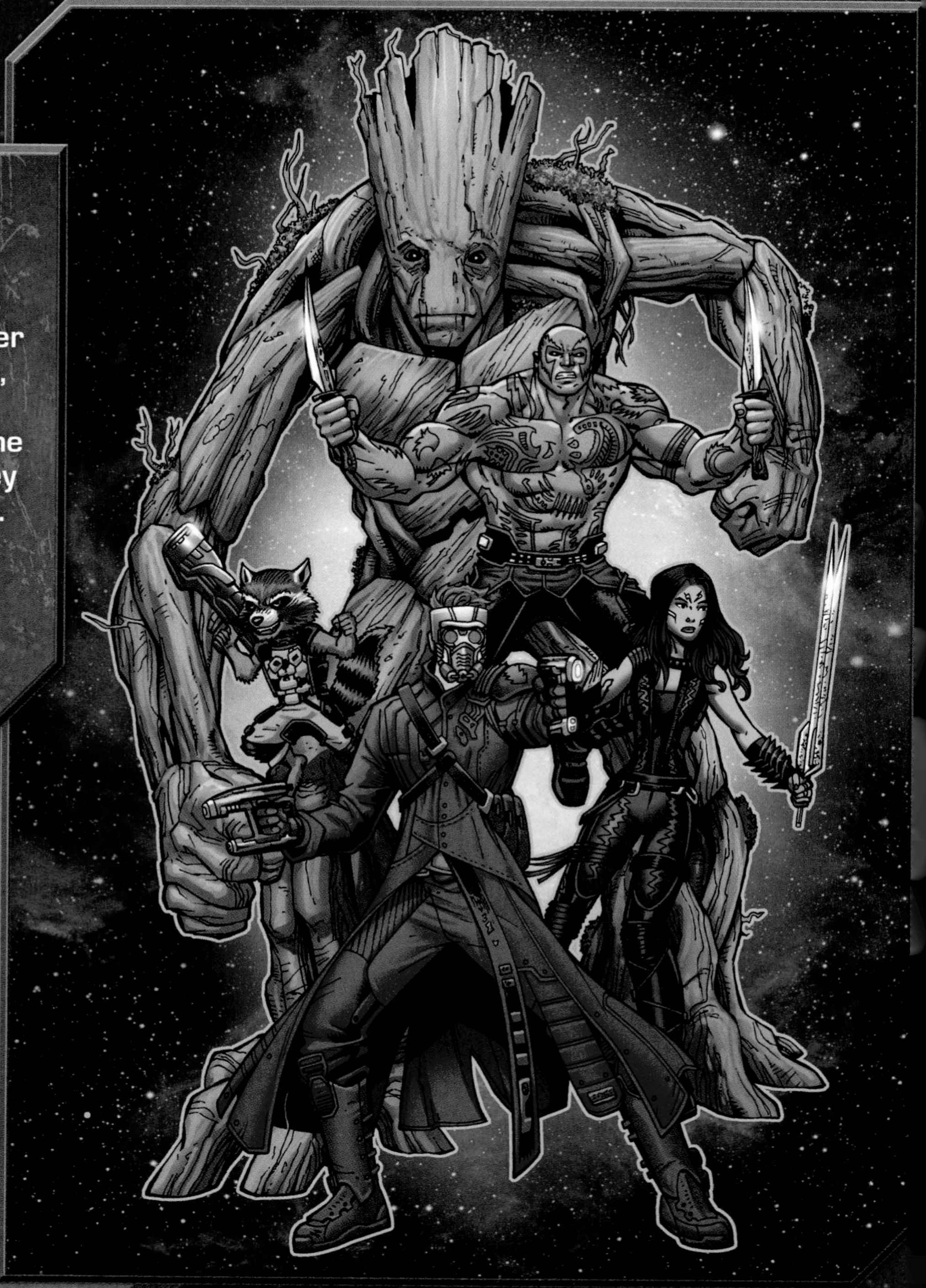